CW00920489

Regards
Ron Fenneley
1998.

MY FRIEND THE PRINCE

Ron Fereday

Illustrations by Jim Smillie

MINERVA PRESS
LONDON
MONTREUX LOS ANGELES SYDNEY

MY FRIEND THE PRINCE
Copyright © Ron Fereday 1997

ISBN 1 86106 665 1

First Published 1997 by
MINERVA PRESS
195 Knightsbridge
London SW7 1RE

Printed in Great Britain for Minerva Press

MY FRIEND THE PRINCE

By the same author:

The Three Faces of Spirit
published by Regency Press.

'The Reducing Mind'
published in *A Lasting Calm*, by the International Library of Poetry.

...sitting upon his pillow, a brown spider.

Jeremy was very **restless** in his bed. Somehow his sleep had been **disturbed**. He thought at first it was his **imagination** playing tricks, but now he was certain that a voice was quietly calling his name.

"Jeremy, Jeremy," it said.

'It is no good,' he thought, 'I shall have to switch my light on.' He put out his hand and pressed the switch of his Mickey Mouse bedside lamp. As his eyes got used to the light, he could see a brown-coloured spider sitting on his pillow. At first it gave him quite a surprise, but he soon forgot this because once again the little hairy **creature** was speaking to him.

"Hello Jeremy, do you remember me? I am the spider you saved from drowning. I fell into the washing-up water in the sink. I had been climbing up the kitchen window."

Jeremy put his face a little closer to the spider.

"Thank you for putting me into that empty matchbox. The cotton wool you covered the bottom of the box with, soaked up all the wet and helped me to get dry and warm again."

Jeremy smiled at his new friend. "You do look well again. I was happy to see you had been able to leave the little bed I had made for you. Where did you go?" he asked.

The little **creature** replied, "When I **recovered**, it took me very little time to drop to the floor and walk home again."

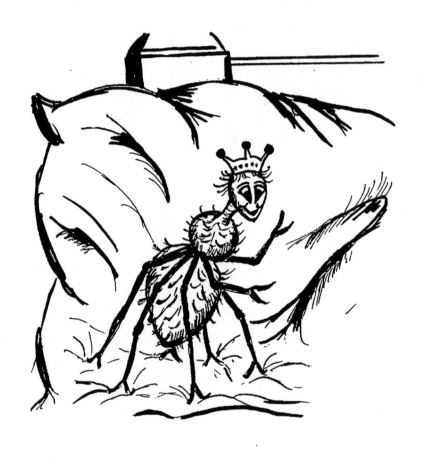

"My name is Redips, Prince Redips."

The young boy was very excited that he could hear the spider and understand what it was saying. Why his long-legged friend was visiting at this time soon became plain.

"My father is the King of Spiders in this house. He is giving a party in your honour, because you saved my life." Raising his two front legs he **continued**, "Will you come with me please?"

"I certainly will," said Jeremy, "but aren't I too big to go with you?"

His little friend said he could **arrange** for Jeremy to be the same size as himself. They would be able to travel together under the floor beneath the clothes cupboard which was in the corner of the bedroom. This made Jeremy even more excited.

The boy remembered that his mother and father always needed to know when he **intended** to wander off and play, so he wrote a short letter on one of the pages of his notebook. This he placed upon his pillow. It read, "I am going to play with my friend, the Prince of Spiders."

"What is your name?" Jeremy asked, putting his face very close to the **creature**. His breath almost blowing his friend off the pillow.

"My name is Redips! Prince Redips," answered his friend.

The boy, **preparing** himself for the adventure which was to come, quickly realised that Redips spelt Spider backwards.

Whoosh! Jeremy was as small as Prince Redips

Tucking his pyjama top inside his trouser bottoms he cheerfully exclaimed, "I am ready to go to the party now, so lead the way Redips, my royal playmate."

"First we must shrink you down to size. Place one of your fingers on the pillow and I will pour a drop of magic liquid on it."

Jeremy followed his friend's **instructions**. The spider **approached** the outstretched finger and seemed to tickle it with one of his front claws. The boy felt an icy cold **sensation** on his finger tip. Immediately, inside his head it seemed as though it were bonfire night all over again. For a brief second there were flashes of light and streams of colour similar to rockets and Roman candles shooting about in a sky. Then, – whoosh! Jeremy was as small as Prince Redips.

At first it was a little frightening to be side by side with a spider as large as himself. The Prince was very good looking, in a strange sort of way.

He laughed at his human friend, "It seems that we have made our first mistake Jeremy. We have to get you from the bed to the floor. Had you been on the floor before you were made smaller, we would not have had this problem."

Both friends were **bemused**. "I have the answer," **continued** Redips, "climb onto my shoulders, as though you are having a piggyback ride."

...similar to Tarzan swinging in the trees.

When Jeremy had settled himself into position, his spider friend attached a thread which he normally used to make his web, to the duvet on the bed. "Hold tight my friend," he cried, and they slowly slipped over the side. Lower and lower they went.

"Whee-ee," Jeremy shouted as he enjoyed the **experience**. He thought Tarzan must have felt like this, swinging in the trees of the jungle. "That was fun," he giggled as they arrived on the carpet with a gentle, plop!

"Follow me Jeremy," Prince Redips called as he made his way to the clothes cupboard and walked behind it. His friend was close on his heels.

*

They **journeyed** beneath the floorboards and in between a maze of brickwork and cracks. Gradually they **descended** through these nooks and crannies until reaching an area which contained a large group of spiders and other **creatures**.

Jeremy and the Prince walked towards the figure of a large brown and cream striped spider. It was the father of Redips. It was the King!

From his position **adjacent** to the crowd he called to the two friends. "Come in Master Jeremy, my **subjects** and my friends are all pleased to meet you on this happy occasion."

Jeremy was soon striding up and down the pitch with the rest of them.

Twenty or thirty little faces looked toward the boy and cheered. "Come and join us in a game of push-ball," one of the crowd called to him as a set of goal posts was **erected** on either side of the room. Prince Redips was voted captain of one team which included Jeremy, also two other spiders and three ants. The other team was selected by a rather plump black ant who elected to be their captain. He looked around him and chose another much slimmer ant, two large woodlice and three spiders.

The two teams faced each other, prepared to start the game.

Jeremy could not see a ball!

All of a sudden a much smaller woodlouse ran to the centre of the playing space. He immediately curled himself into a ball, his hard crusty skin shining in the light, looking altogether like a little plastic pill.

The rules of the game were quickly explained to Jeremy. The object of the game was to roll the ball into the **opponent's** goal. A player could only take six strides forward with the ball then another team mate had to take over. In the meantime, if the referee blew his whistle during the six strides the player had to change direction. If the player did not **release** the ball after the correct number of strides, or change direction at the time of the whistle, then that was called a foul. A player of the other team always took control of the ball following a foul.

As the players rolled the ball around, a referee stood on the touchline, with his back to the players. He would blow his whistle regularly at his choosing. All this was carried out without him ever knowing which player had the ball, or of their position on the pitch.

In the meantime, a second referee ran amongst the players and at the sound of the whistle he would shout, "Stop!" "Change!" "Foul!" and count the number of strides the player took with the ball.

Jeremy was soon striding up and down the pitch with the rest of them. Once when it was his turn to push the ball, the whistle was sounded three times within his six strides. His legs almost got tied in knots as he changed **directions**.

It did not concern the players if they were winning or not. They enjoyed joining in each time it became their turn to move with the shell-like ball.

A peal of laughter would ring out whenever one of them slipped or caused a foul. An even louder cheer went up as each goal was scored.

Very soon the little legs grew weary and the final whistle blew. That was the signal for two other teams to take to the pitch whilst Jeremy and his friends sat and watched.

The King cheered and waved encouragement to the players, and the crowd joined in with his **enthusiasm**.

Preparations were being made for a different game to take place a little farther down the room.

A straight line had been drawn across the floor.

At one end stood a ginger-brown coloured wireworm. All of its hundreds of legs tensed for a run along the line. Balanced upon its back were six wooden skittles.

"Look up at the ceiling Jeremy." He did and saw above the line, six spiders clinging to the ceiling, each had a thin thread hanging from its body, almost reaching to the ground. "See those little pebbles attached to the ends of each thread?" A spider pointed for the benefit of the human. Jeremy could see them and soon realised they would act as **pendulums** swinging across the floor.

Just as he had thought, two teams of six stood facing each other on each side of the line on the floor. The game commenced as the wireworm, with the skittles balanced on its back, hurried along the line.

Players on one side held a pebble and swung it across the floor in an attempt to knock a skittle from the wireworm's back. Only two were successful. The opposing team then had an opportunity to dislodge the skittles on the return journey along the line.

The young boy, joined by his friend the Prince, tried his luck at the game but he was not very successful. Each time he released the pebble it always seemed too late. The wireworm managed to run past with all skittles intact.

The wireworm, with the skittles balanced on its back, hurried along the line.

Prince Redips got very involved in the efforts to improve his knock down total.

Jeremy decided he would like to explore the home the insects were living in. He walked away unseen by the others and not realising that dangers could lie ahead.

*

Jeremy discovered a gap between two bricks and he walked through the opening.

He was beneath the floorboards of his parents' bedroom. Above his head he could see the wooden planks of the floor, and occasionally there were gaps between them. Through the gaps it was easy to **recognise** the underneath of the floor carpet.

After walking a little distance Jeremy saw a shiny object just a few inches in front of him. "It is a silver ring with jewels all around the sides," he spoke aloud to himself. "I remember my mother speaking of losing a ring from her dressing table, when she and Father were decorating the bedroom. This must be the one. When I go back she will be pleased to know I have found it for her."

"Who is that?"

Jeremy heard the voice which came from the direction of a dark corner.

"It's a silver ring with jewels all round the side."

The sound of his voice had obviously **disturbed** something. He could see a long-legged figure creeping toward him.

"Who are you?" it asked. "Why are you **trespassing** in my kitchen? I shall eat you for my dinner."

Walking towards Jeremy was the largest black spider the boy had ever seen in his life. Its eyes were sparkling at the thought of a tasty meal.

Step by step it moved forward. Step by step Jeremy moved backwards, keeping his eyes on the massive **creature**. With each movement the boy grew more scared because the spider was enormous.

It licked its lips and rubbed its tummy.

Suddenly Jeremy could go back no further. He had become stuck in a spider's web!

Closer and closer moved the black spider.

Jeremy could see that it had lost half a leg. 'Probably lost it in a fight of some sort,' the young boy thought. He had never seen a spider without all its eight legs before.

"Help, help," the lad shouted at the top of his voice. How he hoped someone would hear him. "Do not hurt me. I am a friend," he cried to the monster. "Prince Redips is my friend. We were having a party and I got myself lost."

He had never seen a spider without all its eight legs before.

Quickly Jeremy told the story of how he had saved the Prince, and how he was always kind to insects.

The large **creature** believed the story and started to free the boy from the spider's web.

At that moment Prince Redips and a group of searchers appeared through the gap in the wall.

"Seven-and-a-half! Seven-and-a-half! Do not harm my friend." The Prince shouted because he feared the black spider was about to have his playmate for dinner.

Jeremy learned later that 'Seven-and-a-half' was the nickname given to his newly acquired friend because of his having only that number of legs. The spider had once been used as a **plaything** by a young kitten. The missing half of his leg had been broken off during his escape. Ever since then, he had lived all alone and had grown very miserable.

Within a few minutes everyone was happy.

They all said their goodbyes to the lonely spider and returned to the games hall once again.

*

Inside the hall they found the King hastily giving out orders to a number of his **subjects**. A crowd of insects were rushing about the floor. They seemed to be in a panic!

One of the ants told Prince Redips and Jeremy, "Rain water has begun to trickle into the baby nursery room. We have to

23

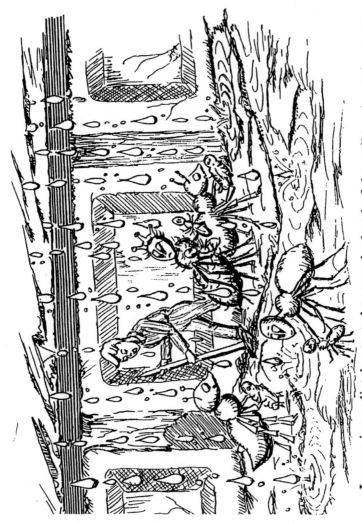

Jeremy immediately started to use the head of the nail to channel a track.

work quickly or the babies will be washed away. They must be moved to higher levels or some may drown."

In the nursery young insects were being carried to and fro by adult ants and spiders.

There was such a great number of them, and Jeremy could see that many of them would die if something was not done more speedily.

Very close to where the rain was coming through the crack in the wall, the young boy picked up a short rusty nail from the floor. It must at some time have been dropped by the builder.

Jeremy immediately started to use the head of the nail to channel a track in the dirt and dust around the nursery floor. The water poured into the groove he made and it was directed to another space in the wall, just like a small river or stream. The rain water then disappeared down the brick wall to the ground below and away from the baby insects.

"Hooray, hooray," all the **creatures** yelled.

"Jeremy has stopped the nursery from being flooded. He has saved the babies. Brave Jeremy."

Only a few of the tiny ones had got wet but they were soon made warm and dry by their mothers and fathers.

"Goodbye Mr Seven-and-a-half." Jeremy waved especially to him.

After the rescue every spider, ant and woodlouse wanted to thank Jeremy and pat him on the back. The King and Prince watched as they all congratulated him and they were both very proud of their human friend.

Speaking to the crowd afterwards, the young spider Prince **concluded**, "So, now my friends you know, boys and girls are not all unkind. They can be our friends if we will let them."

Jeremy and the Prince began to make the return journey to the boy's bedroom. The little hero looked back at the faces of all his new found friends. He waved to them and promised to return again, one day.

At the rear of the crowd he could see the figure of the black spider who was waving happily with everyone.

"Goodbye Mr Seven-and-a-half." Jeremy waved specially to him.

Inside the bedroom the two friends faced each other as they said their goodbye.

"I have had a thrilling time Redips," the boy said.

"So have I," smiled back his young insect friend, "But you must return to your parents and I to my father. Perhaps you would like to visit again sometime?"

"Oh yes. Please Prince Redips." Jeremy gave a little bow, to pay his respects to his royal friend.

They touched hand and claw. Again, as before, Jeremy had flashes of colour in his brain. Whoosh! He was returned to his boy size again. Just in time to see a group of little figures disappear behind his clothes cupboard.

*

"Jeremy, Jeremy, are you getting out of bed young man?"

"Yes Mommy, I am coming."

His mother entered his bedroom just as he remembered to remove the note he had written for her and placed upon his pillow.

"Mommy," he said, looking very concerned, "Do not use a fly spray or anything like that when you clean my room. Please!" Jeremy pleaded. "I have a lot of insect friends it may drive away."

She smiled at him and patted his hair straight across his brow. "If you say so darling. Just to please you."

He walked past his mother in the doorway.

From the bathroom he called to her, "Mommy – do you remember the ring with all the pretty stones in it? You lost it when painting your bedroom. Well, I think if you get the carpet up from the floor, you might find it under the floorboards."

"What made you think of my eternity ring at this time of the morning?" his mother queried.

Jeremy's cheeky face grinned back at him from the mirror, as he brushed his teeth over the washbasin. He thought, 'I'll tell Mommy and Daddy the story of my adventures, – one day!'

Dictionary of Difficult Words

Adjacent	ajj'ay'sent	near at hand, very close
Approached	ap'row'ch'd	moved closer to the finger
Arrange	arr'ain'j	sort out the problem
Bemused	bem'yu'z'd	very deep in thought
Concluded	con'klood'ed	came to end of talk, finishing his talk
Continued	kunt'in'yew'd	he kept on talking
Creature	kreech'er	a living animal
Descended	dess'end'ed	made their way lower
Directions	dy'reck'shun'z	move one way and then another
Disturbed	dist'erb'ed	upset – could not sleep
Enthusiasm	en'thoo'zi'az'm	more feeling than usual, enjoy more
Erected	err'eck'ted	placed upright
Experience	ex'peer'ee'ens	the feeling of the moment
Imagination	imaj'in'ay'shun	fantasy – thought he was dreaming
Instructions	instruk'shun's	telling his friend what to do
Intended	int'end'ed	made up his mind to do something
Journeyed	jern'eed	made their way, walked along a path
Opponent	opp'owe'nent'z	in the other team

Pendulums	pen'doo'lum'z	swinging one way and then another
Preparing	prep'air'ing	making himself ready, thinking of things to come
Recognise	reck'og'n'eye'z	make out, know what it is
Recovered	rek'uv'er'd	got back his health
Release	re'lees	let go of
Restless	rest'less	on the move, kept moving his arms and legs
Sensation	sens'ay'shun	a funny feeling on his finger tip
Subjects	sub'jeck'tz	under control of the King
Trespassing	tress'pass'ing	being where you should not be without permission